THE CAMPHOR OF NIGHT

ODE TO AN UNFINISHED COIN

This day, today, when looked at from the window of future, wouldn't it seem golden? But today it feels like just another day. Why does all this preciousness have to pass to be seen? Why can't it get its due while it lives.

Unfortunately that's the way it has always been.

The future seems to hold a certain value for the past.

But present seems to be like an unfinished coin. It's still incomplete, to derive any worth.

The poems in this collection 'The Camphor of Night' are little things I stole from life which found their way to a treasury box in which they lay locked for years until I realized these stolen things have a life of their own and hence they need to be set free because now is their time to breathe.

Things I stole from life
Lie buried
In pages of this book

Second Edition : September 2019

ISBN : 978-93-86619-30-3

Publisher :   Anybook
                G - 248, 2nd Floor
                Sector - 63
                Noida - 201301
                Cell : 9971698930
                E-mail contactanybook@gmail.com
                Website www.anybook.org

The Camphor of Night

A poetry collection by SAMIR SATAM

Cover Design : Yaseen Anwer
Book Design : Anybook
Photograph on Cover: © Samir Satam

© Samir Satam

The Camphor of Night

Samir Satam

Poetry

Self-Introduction of an Introvert:

I live in a little corner, by my own rules, on my own terms, my own set of personalized morals. Here in this little place, I have my own garden where pastel thoughts bloom. Time flows at my pace. There is a little door that opens in an exotic village named Past. I visit that village often, stay there as long as I like.

The books I have read over the years, the films I have watched. They hug a wall, ready to spring a quote or two whenever I need them. Or flash a scene when I yearn to go back to one of my favourite films.

The tastes and aromas hang in air, fresh as they were when I first met them. Here I still feel the traces of people I loved. I can smell the bouquet of fragrances of their skins, of their words, of their thoughts, of their ways of loving me.

It's a comfort to have an ever growing world of my own within this world and a luxury to be able to spend time in it. I have developed a certain hobby to derive from the outer world and store things in my corner.

So used to I am to this place that, where ever I go I carry my corner with me...

To,
Saanvi, Aaira, Aarya, Atharva., Vihaan & Saanjh..

Along with all those little ones
Who are yet to discover the world…
And
For the rest of us grown-ups
Who have turned into,
Broken Little Beautiful Things

Contents

Drifting Souls

You,
My friend,
My mirror image…
So much like me…
Yet,
My most brutal critic!

<u>*blues*</u>

LEAF

Decaying amongst dry twigs,
Melancholy leaf sings,
Songs of a life green

LEFT BEHIND

There are stories.
Beneath pieces of clothing,
Left behind at lovers' homes;
A Jacket, A Shawl,
A Shirt, A Handkerchief,
Inner Wear, Inner Scars,
All go to the same laundry…
…of scented memories.

A LOVER

A lingering thought…
Of the one I love
But will never have,
Fills me with a frenzy

Of a thirsty ocean
Under a dark cloud,
Of a hungry wolf
Under a shepherd's axe,

A wait as long as
Death,
An existence as long as
Silence,

Of a lingering thought
That leaves me in reminiscence
Of the one I love too much,
To have...

A PHOTOGRAPHER

Eventually
As a photographer,
I failed,
My camera couldn't
Love anyone else...

STOLEN

I,
I keep looking,
I keep looking...

...for a smile hidden in your eyes,
For a poem scribbled in air between us,
And when I find them in the way you look at him...

I,
I stare,
I stare more and more intently...
...at those little things stolen from my home...

LONER

If you look deep enough in eyes of a loner,
Beneath the brave smile you may discover,
Ruins of a broken home...
...haunted by ghosts of dreams

APARTMENT

We roamed around looking for our apartment,
You kept bothering the agent for a road facing
view,
It didn't matter to me much then,
At the sound of my reluctance,
You mocked me for being an introvert

While we unpacked on the first night,
You switched off the light,
Pinned me against the window
Enveloped me between your thighs,
We made love above a clueless city...

Today as I sit on the window sill,
Feet of lost times hanging above the city,
I keep looking down at vehicles, people,
Of you crossing the road below,
I shudder at the thought.

Now I wish I hadn't listened to you;
How I wish I hadn't given in,
To every whim of your nomadic heart;
I would not be waiting for you,
Were it not a road facing apartment!

THE LETTERS KEEP ACCUMULATING

The birds have flown,
Leaving the nest dusty and dry,
Even friends don't drop by these days,
The house is on its own,
But at the door,
The letters keep accumulating...

Why would someone write to an empty house?
At home are just the ghosts of times spent here,
Locked in the confines of their own existence,
Breathing in a vast emptiness,
Living and re-living bits and pieces of a life that
was...
I wish those silly ghosts could read letters...

But no, they don't,
So while they go on living in there,
The letters lie on the floor,
Bewildered, Confused,
Hoping to be picked up some day,
Dreaming to be read,
The letters keep accumulating...

BLACK BUTTER

Don't burden me with love,
For I have drunk the night,
That we churned out gently,
From between our brushing skins,
Till the breathless moon
Almost died of melancholy,

Don't burden me with love,
As it may fade and die slowly,
While the first drop of dawn
Burns away tender dreams of night,
But the buttery darkness sticks
To the slippery skin of my soul.

HOPELESS

Clueless…
While she goes on with her life,
He keeps carving her name,
In the mist that settles on windows,

In the mist that settles on windows,
He keeps carving her name,
While she goes on with her life,
Clueless…

TRUTH

The labour in uttering the truth,
Gives birth to a stutter in your tongue,
You need not agonize yourself thus,
For hesitation too is an expression...

> Guilt accumulates,
> Heart erupts,
> Truth flows...

While vast fields of life are being searched,
Truth stays hidden in nuances

> ...Truth is all I want,
> Truth is all I fear...

INDIGO

Indigo evening floods the city,
To unleash ghosts of time
When we were on the same side,
Of moist eyelids… In pastel hued dreams…

Today you have crossed,
The bridge to reality,
To a world of duties, expenses,
And green comfort of money,

In my wallet full of dreams,
Currencies are homeless refugees,
I agree, your reality is real,
So are the blues of my dreams…

OBSOLETE

I reached as usual,
Late...
Empty-handed...
With a few things obsolete,
A throat full of heart,
A heart full of regret,
That out of embarrassment,
I couldn't spill on your grave...

ANSWERS

Some questions
Have demons for answers,
That rise over the city of curiosity
To drink squashed red dreams
From cracked bowls of broken hearts

A CLAUSE

Death, I wouldn't mind
If Love is promised
On the other side

HOMESICKNESS

No matter how far you go,
There's this homesickness
That keeps tugging at your heart,
To come back...
        ...not to your wardrobe and refrigerator,
           But wherever that one person is...
                Because,
           Home is never about roof and walls?

BUT HOW?

I must have the moon,
And to see it with my eyes,
I must have the gloom
Multiplied in a million mirrors,

But unlike light,
Darkness doesn't reflect,
Denying us a peep
In its mysteries,

Unlike Life,
Death doesn't reflect,
Denying us a peep
Into afterlife

I must have the moon,
But how?

<u>*the language of love*</u>

NAME

On the nape of your name,
Is a poem of my breath,
That teases my tongue,
To fly off my lips,
With a promise of a kiss...

On the wrist of your name,
Is a fragrance of rain,
That floats in my dreams,
Like something as temporary,
And as permanent as a flower

INSPIRATION

Somewhere in cobbled streets of Paris,
A lone musician on the sidewalk knows not,
That love took birth in a room upstairs,
Kindled by the tune he played...

LONG DISTANCE RELATIONSHIP

Let's sit on the porch,
You on yours, Me on mine;
Let's talk…
The wind will carry on its back,
Our conversations across oceans,
When our words meet,
Is it possible for them to not kiss?

OH! AIR…

Like a traveller's soul stuck in a latched room,
I gasp for breath in clutch of distance's gloom,
Oh Air… Go… Tease my beloved's hair,
For I am far and she is dour...

MISSING PIECE

When the doorbell rings
I already know who it is,
Fatigued…
…after a long day at work,
Straight into my arms,
Here comes my missing piece

TO MY GIRLFRIEND'S LOVER

Like me, you seem to love her too…
Tempting though it is,
I won't get into an argument
Over who loves her more…
I simply hope we both love her enough…

SUNSET

And when the sun goes down,
I look towards you for sunshine

DEBT

---

all the love that i owe you,
stays hidden beneath my skin,
with no way for it to rise to my eyes,
it stays buried alive, breeding,
fermenting in its own yearning,
seeping deep in my core,
for all the love that i owe you,
sprouts beneath my skin,
with no space for it to bloom...
...i have flowered into something like Love

LOVE AT FIRST SIGHT

Her eyes linger on my skin,
Unaware of what they do to me,
She smiles…

…that's when,
I start making arrangements...
...to go stay on the moon.

FLAWS

____

As you stand there,
Your secrets uncovered,
Your soul naked,
Your blunders visible,
I wonder,
Am I falling...
...In love with your flaws?

ES MUSS SEIN

All the restlessness of wandering feet
Find shelter in shadows of her
remembrances,
That are warmer than her
presence ever was,

All his dreams now revolve within him,
All his songs now fly to sing of his
dreams,
And his wandering feet tap, tap, tap to
his songs,

He floats on waves of an unpredictable
wind,
If there is something that keeps him so,
It must be... It must be...

*(Inspired by central theme of Milan
Kundera's 'The Unbearable Lightness Of
Being')*

ROMANCE

Under the starry sky,
By the river,
A bench, two people,
Whispering… Conversing…

Night breathes
Alive in its solitude,
Tiptoes past them,
Looking… Smiling…

At two souls
Naked in thoughts,
Words intimate,
Pouring… Touching…

A bench, two people,
By the river,
Under the starry sky,
Blushing… Living…

ONCE UPON A NIGHT

Once upon a night,
The moon sang to stars,
They smiled with twinkling eyes,
You and I were stardust bright,
Glowing in silver of moonlight,

Unaware of our ticking watches
We talked, smiled, laughed,
Teased the sky till it blushed,
Tickled the sea with our feet,
And let the sand caress our cheeks

In the corners of your lips
Were arcs of a merry night,
Could have kissed you then,
But we let the moment pass,
Blending in shadows of time...

SILENT LOVE

When we meet,
I dare not look at you,
There's no place on you
That doesn't tempt me,
To steal a kiss,
So I sit there…
Silent…
Looking somewhere else,
While you talk
About other things…

HOLDING HANDS

We forgot to hold hands,
Today...
...other thoughts played on our minds

I LOVE...

I love the colours
That blush my cheeks,
When I see you in my room,

I love the song
That plays in my ears,
While I hear you breathe,

I love the quills
That run in my hair,
While I draw you close,

I love the verse
That appears on my skin,
While I nibble on your lips,

I love the shapes
That shiver beneath my fingers,
While I undo your dress,

I love the violence
That erupts in my pores,
While I invade your core,

I love the rhythm
That dances in my veins,
While I enter your depths,

I love the flavour
That lingers in my mouth,
While I moan your name,

I love the fragrance
That dwells in my senses,
When I wake in your arms...

WHILE YOU SLEEP

While I watch you sleep,
I lose my senses
To the little storm
That conjures in the depth
At the base of your throat,

As lines brew on your forehead,
Between your eyes,
Then ease in smoothness of your skin,
I wonder what storms
Rise and fall in your dreams...

UNAWARE

People at war
And
People in love,
Are unaware
Of other mishaps...

SHARED SILENCE

In silences shared
Between two people
Snuggle songs of comfort,

In silences shared
Between two people
Sail seasons of expressions,

In silences shared
Between two people
Dwell depths of friendship,

When all is spent,
When all is lived,
These silences will sing…

FEAR

I won't ask any questions,
I am afraid, you may lie,
I am afraid, you won't

<u>*drifting souls*</u>

DON'T TELL ME…

No, don't tell me your name,
First let our bodies introduce each other,
Fingers, skins, cheeks, lips, tongues,
Forearms, calves, thighs, sighs...
Let our bodies find comfort in warmth,
And then if either of us doesn't want to run,
Maybe we will exchange names, numbers, lives…

TOGETHER

I know, together we can never live,
But together, we can leave,
At sigh of our last breath,
Our bodies one with soil,
When we are free,
From all distractions of life,
We will make our bed,
In the lost vessel of a broken dream...

THE LIAR

Now that nothing matters,
You must know,

I never lied to you
About my myths,

I did lie to you
About my truths...

A CONVERSATION

To each other...
...we spoke in facts,
Air between us dense with a stink of truth,
Lacking the illusionary scent of passions,
Stagnant - Our Conversation, Our Relation,
How could we go on then?
On crutches of honesty we walked away,
From all that we built,
From all that we shared…

EMPTINESS

The plane flies away with you,
And so does something I owned,
Your bag must feel heavy today,
My city feels stripped off its soul...

BAGGAGE

My bag rattles on airport tiles,
With an impotent yearning
To stay back in your city,
Ruthlessly I drag it,
Along with my heart…

TRYING…

In chill of a reckless night,
After making love to a stranger,
I pull over a quilt of your thoughts,

And lit up a cigarette,
To see your face in smoke,
Of my burning heart,

The cruel joke,
In trying to forget you is...
...it takes me back to you…

UNSAID

A creature of yearning pounces to devour,
Meek memories, of things you said to me,
And of things you never said to me,
Yet the later rise from ashes of past,
For love to grow into my own personal monster
Some words must stay unsaid...

ONE NIGHT STAND

In a hotel room,
For a single night,
One doesn't unpack all…

TO MY HEALER

You have always been my healer;
That's why I keep going on and on,
Through tresses of unknown nights,
To get my heart broken over and over,
So that you can mend it again and again...

FOR GRANTED

Holding hands, A casual kiss,
The brush of your hand,
Softness of your breasts,
A hug when I need,
To snuggle in a corner,
Sex on a wintry night,
I wish, I could take these for granted,
Only if you had married me...

GHOST

You walk out, I walk out,
We admit… with each other, we are done,
Questions and answers are none,
No love, no expectations,
Then what is it that lingers?
For years after you are gone,
Out of nowhere, in middle of a game,
While dining at our favourite restaurant,
Even on a date with another woman,
In my bed, when I sleep,
Invisible threads drag it in my dreams,
It rises and jumps all over,
From haunted corners of my mind,
I wonder; has it come to visit you yet?
The Ghost of our dead relationship?

ILLUSION

Dreaming of a fresh start,
Of moving to a different city,
Of building a life from scratch,
I forget it's the same old me,
As long as it's the…
…Same…
…Old,…
…Me…
…a fresh start is but an illusion…

FORGETTING

At the edge of age,
He took a vacation
To the land of forgetting,
One by One…
Each strand of memory,
That kept his heart burning,
Hence beating,
Hence alive,
When he felt her name leave,
He forgot the art of breathing...

FORGIVE ME…

___

An intoxicating twilight breeze
Blends with music of breaths,
In hurried steps on cobbled streets,

Intimate smiles aromatic with longing
Beneath clear skies cloaked in clouds of day-
dreams,
Give birth to apparitions of rains in warm
evenings,

Under a reckless tender gaze on unexplored skin
Looms a damp chuckling voice of a violent kiss,
Yet the wait is more bittersweet than the meet,

So forgive me if this kiss doesn't find a place
In my amorphous country of reminiscence,
As my last days are spent in a lost city of reverie...

Also forgive me if I choose to live
In an untidy memory of my satisfying stutter,
Instead of a cosy cottage of fluent expressions...

And forgive me if I hurt you by denying a kiss,
Just so that I could never forget the anticipation,
Which has stayed with me ever since...

*(First featured in 'The Garden of Poetry and Prose',
where the poet was invited to write as a guest poet)*

SHIVERS

In those moments,
When I think,
Of his lips on yours...
His skin against yours...
...Little deaths,
Of something I felt once,
Arrive...
...to stay in shivers of my petty heart...

POISON OF PROMISES

Say you love me,
Say you don't...
But I deny to take,
The poison of your promises,
For there's no bigger betrayal,
In world of words...

<u>*waiting room*</u>

NEVER ENOUGH

Since his death, he spent his time,
Staring in her eyes, waiting…
For her to see him, to feel him;
All he got was a stray drop of salt,
Trickling from corners of a lost gaze,
But tears like love are never enough...

THE STORY CONTINUES...

At every point that I thought
Was a concluding moment,
The story laughed at me,
And went on flowing
Like a vicious wind of rumours;
Flows through small towns
With fluidity of junk music…

DELIVERED

From this porch of Nowhere,
All that I shred from myself
And offer to the wind,
Will come to you in bursts of breeze,
When you breathe in a fraction of me,
I will consider myself delivered.

<u>*individualism*</u>

FLOWERS

I pay not for flowers,
But for transportation,
For efforts involved
In bringing them to me,
Flowers can't be bought,
They are their own...

GREY

I am lawful, unlawful,
A duty, A fault,
A virtue, A sin,
A day, A night,
I am as vast as I am minuscule,
As human as I am inhuman,
As pure as I am impure,
My darkness gives birth
To all that illuminates in me,
At peace with my blacks and whites,
I am an ever varying shade of grey

BEING YOURSELF

At some point,
Comes a time,
When you are no more
The man they expect you to be,
The man whom his relationships define,
The man who hides his desires,
When you can finally be what you truly are...
Free...
Then you know,
You have arrived...

TENDERNESS

Never mistaken tenderness in a man as his
weakness,
That he can afford to be gentle in a harsh world,
Must tell you something
Of his internal demons he has fought and caged

MUSK

Musk sets a deer apart from its herd,
In quest of fragrance, strays crazed,
Craving for a thing that stays within,
Poetry does the same to a poet

<u>*harsh realities*</u>

HOSPITALS

Hospitals like airports smell,
Of tears, fears, prayers,
Of helpless wails,
Of restless smiles,
At departures and arrivals,
Of dreams spent,
Of lives yet to unfold,

Hospitals like airports swell
With duty-free shopping bags,
Of gifts discharged from beds,
Of sleeps ripened to never wake,
A few bags of deeds checked-in,
A few bags of possibilities delivered,
On rolling belts, waiting to be claimed...

WHORE

Layers
of make-up,
cheap clothes,
fake jewellery,
self-forced smiles,
tobacco stained teeth,

Layers and Layers of
impudence,
starvation,
abuse,
stink of alcohol,
pennies earned,

And at her core
flickers,
glows,
something dull yet pure,
which her layers keep covered,
a golden ball of grief...

A WHORE'S SAVINGS

Above everything else, she saved,
A few abusive words in her breath
Bred in her need of bread,
And a few crumpled notes in her pouch
Fragrant with memories of someone's touch,
To spend those she could never afford...

BACK HOME

Here at my adopted home
A cool breeze is a feast
While back home
We used to waltz in snow

Our birth place brims with,
Old world charm of houseboats,
A Dal with shikaras afloat
Like mist on dreamy eyelids

Kahwa sipped
on lazy afternoons,
In the chill of the night,
Moon shimmers over the valley

Then came a season of nightmares
Of loud speakers vomiting hatred…
Of abductions, gang rapes…
Of young and old massacred…

As memories drift
from white of snow to red of blood,
I take solace
in an occasional cool breeze of my adopted home

(On exodus of Kashmiri Pandits)

MANNEQUINS

We are mannequins in a showcase of this world
Flaunting our morals, ideologies, religions, lives,
Passively, and sometimes actively, pushing others
To think like us, to live like us,
Letting these tools make fools of us,
By making us stand wearing their wares,
To con others in joining our make-believe world,
See, what evolution made of us!
Just mannequins in a showcase of this world!

COMMUNAL RIOTS

Dark is the colour
Of dried blood,
But the blindfolds of religion
Are thicker, murkier,

Someone was gang raped
While her husband
Was made to watch,
Both then burnt alive,

Someone, I hear,
Was chopped,
But first his kids
Were shredded to pieces

Someone served his own sisters
With poisoned milk,
When their killers broke the door
They found the dead smiling, taunting,

I hide beneath my bed
While on my skin
Stories crawl,
Written in night's ink

IN THE WAY

Kids play cricket
In the midst of victory cries
And sighs of defeat,
The ball goes whoosh…
Higher than ever…
Into a tree…

Comes down crashing
A nest with its eggs
While a birdie flies to another tree
Looking down at a home that was
It flutters around in despair
Not knowing who to blame

Who is actually to be blamed?
Kids are supposed to play
Balls are supposed to fly
It's the nest that came in the way
The bird looks on,
Its world destroyed

I wonder,
These floods, earthquakes,
That sweep away civilizations,
Are we just in the way
Of something larger,
Beyond our sense of sight!

LEADERS

Real Leaders enable people to think rationally,
To erase religion, caste, creed based divisions
and
Drive them towards co-existence,
Making room for a country to prosper...

All this in service of the people...

Whereas,

Opportunist fascists who wear masks of Leaders,
Use religion to widen rifts and gain power,
and
Once in power, they fool people in believing,
"Everything is fine", while letting violence breed,
In minds, on social media and eventually in
streets...

All this in name of the nation...

GUILTY

When popular leaders give backdoor entry
To religious and ideological extremists,
To cultivate an environment
Ripe with hatred and killings,
While making the educated voters blind
With grand development plans,
It's nothing short of open bribery
To cover up mass-murders,
And if we keep looking away from dead bodies
With dreamy eyes towards clean, sparkling
roads,
Then we too have blood on our hands...

*(For all those helpless victims lynched in the name of
cow.)*

<u>*cityscape*</u>

SHRINKING CITY

The city asks,
How many hungry souls
Can One-Room Kitchen hold?

A LOST CITY

I can barely recognize this city,
The poem I slid below her door
Is lost in grime of time,
The girl who lived in that home
Is lost in streets of memory,
Without her, without my poem,
It's not the same,
I can barely recognize this city…

CONSTIPATED CITY

Dense rains, flooded lanes
High tide, Drain-Gates close,
Sky cries, Sea roars,
People swim, Vehicles float,
Stairs drown, Ceilings leak,
On ground floors, utensils float,
Umbrellas here, Raincoats there,
Water doesn't seem to care,
Morning knees, Afternoon waists,
By evening, it's time for necks,
Empty trains, Platforms full,
Passengers none, Prisoners all,
A place that never stops
Today is on a pause,
Waiting to be relieved,
A city constipated…

<u>*unaccustomed*</u>

THOUGHTS

Thoughts are ghosts,
They travel across time
To haunt solitary people
Unknown to each other...

Everything that we are thinking now has been thought
by someone long before us...
Everything that we are thinking now will be thought
by someone else after us...

ICEBERG

Singing without music,
Talking without words,
Are like icebergs...
So much is beneath,
Of what is possibly heard...

MOTHER'S HEART

Am talking about that mother's heart,
Whose husband and son,
Are fighting at dinner table,
It's mostly torn between duty and love,
Worse, sometimes between duty and duty,
Blessed are those mothers,
Whose hearts are torn,
Between love and love

CANDLES

Little electric bulbs that act as candles,
Lack the vulnerability of originals,

They lack the adventure of flame,
Illuminating and dangerous at the same time,

They lack the scent of wax,
Melting under the love of a burning wick,

Little electric bulbs that look like candles,
Lack the bittersweet taste of a short life…

UNWRITABLE

Poetry is unwritable,
I say it again...
It's livable, but unwritable

You change your baby's diapers
While your boss hurls unpleasantries over the
phone,

You stumble out of a loveless marriage,
And love yourself in ways your partner couldn't

While your partner looks for his own pieces
In a maze to rebuild his own dreams

In holding your father's hand to support him
The way he held yours when you were young,

In walking the streets of an unknown city
To see what the locals take for granted,

And then to go back to your own city
And look for things you had overlooked

In that solitary moment of your vacation
When you finally get to talk to yourself

Poetry is scattered in all such moments,
How is it possible to write it?
Verses are just fragments of what we feel..

MOONLIGHT

I carved a piece of moonlight,
And folded it in my wallet,
In shape of a poem,
I will unfold it on a darker night,
To let its silver drench me again,
In a cool embrace…

MOON-DUST

Ogling women,
Poetry spouting poets,
Wonder shining in eyes of a kid,
Cities drenched in cool silver,
Moon-dust sparkling on water
And sprinkled to the wind,
All the beauty that he is worth,
Will he ever find his significant other?
Or will the moon always stay single?

<u>*music*</u>

PRIVATE MUSIC

Lovers & Loners
Sway to music
Inaudible to others...

EARPHONES

Hard rock, Bass guitar, my earphones streamed...
When she caught sight of me,
She was saying something,
Something, I can't be sure of,
I remember one thing though,
Music... I saw... playing on her face
In lines on her forehead,
In the redness of her cheeks,
The way she bit her lip,
The way she grit her teeth,
It was there, it might still surface if you mention me,
My earphones streamed bass guitar... hard rock...
While I watched on her face,
The music that played...

TUNE THAT PLAYS ON HIS MIND

Unable to find an outlet,
To the tune that plays on his mind,
He writes numerous pieces,
When he is done with all the papers,
He starts scribbling tunes on walls,
Now his home is filled with music,
But one piece is still missing,
The tune that plays on his mind…

FRENCH

Dear France,
    Your language to me is music,
    I don't understand a word,
    But I stand dumbstruck as you talk,
    While I feel my heart waltz

SONG

Let it rise and fall,
Let it beat its feet in air,
Let the music raise a storm
On dry plateau of my heart,
Take away my boat,
Take away my home,
But let the tune stay,
All I have is this song

<u>*nomads*</u>

HEARTBREAKER

I break a bit each time I break a heart,
I smile to make it easier to hate me,
How do I explain? It's not so easy,
They must understand, I have to do it anyway,
I have to run, I have to leave while the night is
dark,
They wouldn't know but I will think of them,
And hope that they will find what they are looking
for,
Pieces of me that I get left behind
Might find their ways to thrash cans,
Soon the tides will wash me away,
But I will continue looking on…
I will continue looking on
For the one who can break my heart,
I won't hate her though,
As, I know what it takes to break…

DILEMMA

Playing on planes of my skin
A thousand urges of desire.

In lanes of my mind
Songs of melancholy

In warmth of body
Breathes a crushed soul

The night looks on
Silently, smiling sadistically,

While I struggle to make sense
Of the place I am in...

...in bed with a woman
Thinking of another!

TEARS OF A WOMAN

She hurls tears to the wind
And create oceans of cravings
In hearts of men who will stay
A bit crazed, A bit sane,
But never the same ever again,
For the mist in her eyes is born,
From death of a thousand worlds within...

BUTTERFLY

If I agree to stay,
What do I tell the butterfly in me?
The one with a short life and colourful dreams,
That rise beyond boundaries of sane norms,
To kiss flowers of love and freedom,
And other things considered lame in this world,
Like smiles that germinate on vagabond lips,
On discovering something as simple and as complex
As an unseen colour that caresses a shy sky,
For dreams are not just dreams,
But a struggling flutter to free one's wings,
So, if I agree to stay while it yearns to fly,
What do I tell the butterfly in me?

TOURIST

A local would never understand,
The addiction to pain of an ever-leaving nomad,
Who in turn will never understand,
The warm comfort of a town's cocoon,
For France is far, and Paris is no home,
And grapes of Bordeaux are sour,
For he will never walk those vineyards,
But will only sip pain from a glass
Full of crushed fruit of soil he yearns to eat,
Like a child with dreams foiled...

GROWING UP...

____

Think of those rivers of tears
In which we enter to bathe,
To walk out a little grown up
And a little bit dead

FADING AWAY

Drop by Drop, Breath by Breath,
Each experience that gives us a bit,
Takes a little of us with it;
An angel's share,
From casks of our bodies,
Evaporates...

Life is a process of fading away,
Continuously... Consistently...
While arriving aren't we departing?
From some place to somewhere else!
While living aren't we dying?
One millisecond at a time!

Evaporates,
From casks of our bodies,
An angel's share...
Takes a little of us with it,
Each experience that gives us a bit,
Drop by Drop... Breath by Breath...

Art
Is a love child
Of Restlessness and Insanity

Acknowledgements

There are people in our lives whom we cherish for just being themselves. We know some of these people deeply, while some we know by their work and yet we feel we have known them through the experiences they share and then there are a few people, who just come into our lives with a whole shipload of kindness and unload it in our courtyard while we are left short of words to thank them enough for the warmth they spread.

'The Camphor of Night' caught it`s first ray of daylight when Yaseen Anwer *(founder of Kaafiya)* asked me one evening to compile my stray poems and send them across to him. I remember I was sitting in a cafe named 'Chocolaterie Beluga' hidden in a little lane in Munich at that moment. As I hold this book in my hand, everything about that evening comes back to me. Yaseen's gesture born out of his benevolence, his way of making a person feel special blended with the ambience of that chocolaterie and the taste of the hotchocolate I was sipping... Everything blends together in a memory that brings back that evening in form of this book. I won`t say, "Thank you", Yaseen, as that expression won`t be enough.

Sadia Khan *(Poet, In My Patina Cup)* has been an integral part of this book ever since it was first compiled.

She has been as kind as she has been brutal towards molding a few shapeless poems in this collection into a shape that reveals only as muchas is needed. Gratitude isn't a protocol between friends, so I will just leave it to that. However, I will always remember your kind gesture, Sadia.

I can only present a heartful of gratefulness to Dr. Ampat Koshy and Rochelle Potkar for taking time to read my manuscript and gifting their first kind words to my book. Nothing boosts confidence in a poet like me, when praise comes from established personalities in the world of literature.

I feel overwhelmed to mention only in fraction of inexpressible ways in which my friends andacquaintances from both near and far – Somya Mehrotra, Anushree Sanzagiri, Devdatta Sanzagiri, Vikram Khanna, Swati Khanna, Pranav Varma, Pallavi Varma, Deepali Yemul, Sai Darshan Bhagat, Divya Nair, Biju Appu, Kabir (Manan) Malik, Neha Krishna have knowingly andunknowingly provided inspiration, motivation and guidance to express in words everything that cannot be said.

A special mention of my brother Nikhil Satam and my parents without whose emotional support I wouldn't have been alive to write these poems.

This book wouldn't have been possible without immense love and support from Parag Agrawal and his team at AnyBook Publishing House.